Matters of the Heart

Inspirational Poems Borne out of Life Experiences

Lurlls

Copyright © 2023 by Lurlls

All rights reserved.

No portion of this book may be reproduced in any form without written permission from the publisher or author, except as permitted by UK & International Services Registration Office of Copyright House Limited.

Illustrations by Lurlls

Dedication

I dedicate this book to the most precious gem in this world, my beautiful mother.
I thank God for this precious gift from heaven.

Contents

1. Whatever — 1
2. What Face do I See? — 3
3. Database — 6
4. When My Door is Shut — 8
5. Anger — 11
6. The Trap — 15
7. My Mountain — 17
8. My Pain — 19
9. When I Am Weak — 22
10. Forgiveness — 24
11. Mind Decay — 26
12. HBRCB — 29

13.	Take The Limits Off	32
14.	Scoff	35
15.	The Graveyard Shift	39
16.	My Heart Says Yes	42
17.	Arrows of Lies	46
18.	Rising Sun	51
19.	What You Hear!	55
20.	3am TTJ	57
21.	Sunday Morning	62
22.	Deep In Despair Jesus Was There	67
23.	Gravel	69
24.	I Almost Let Go	72
25.	Stuck Waiting for Death	75
26.	Dance of the Mind	81
27.	Intrusion	85
28.	Broken Pitcher	88
29.	Charmed By Evil	93

30.	The Crushing	99
31.	Break me Lord	104
32.	Look To God	106
33.	The Poison Tongue	108
34.	Fall in Love	111
35.	Mr Arrogant	115
36.	I Woman	118
37.	Help Me Make It Through The Night	123
38.	Rejected or Protected	127
39.	So Hard	130
40.	It's Complex	132
41.	Welcome To the Safe Space Room	134
42.	Each Time	137
43.	Day One	140
44.	Just a Smile	142
45.	Just One Question!	144
46.	Every Time	146

47.	Love	148
48.	I Want a Rich Man	150
49.	Scrapheap	154
50.	The Sun will Shine Again	157
51.	Sugar Coat	159
52.	Acceleration	164

Whatever

WHATEVER THE WEATHER, my Lord, You are there.

Despite my faults and failures, Lord, You are there.

You made me from dust and to dust, I will return.

I am made in Your Image and I am proud to be Yours.

Whatever the time of day, I can call upon Your Name.

I can brave the storms because Your unseen Hand hovers over me.

It's obvious You care because it's in Your Word.

You will never leave me or forsake me.

Whatever the emotional tide that I may ride, You always give me a crown.

A crown with Your Glory imprinted in gold.

A strength that rises like a sweet aroma, embraces my soul.

Whatever the tyrant of our souls inflicts, during his daily tirades.

I can sit back, when I'm under attack and relax.

Then look him in the eye and say

"WHATEVER"!

What Face do I See?

♥

WHO ARE YOU? THE untouchable, strong jovial you.

The face, as you know, deep down inside, is not true, the untouchable you.

The face that hides the hurt, pain and shame, the untouchable you.

Who are you today?

Do we really see the real you as we walk the road of life.

What is going on deep down inside the untouchable you?

What is real and imagined inside the head of the untouchable you?

Knock, Knock! Will the real you stand up?

How long will you cling to the untouchable you?

Is the pain so great that you bury it deep down inside?

That the light of God will never shine?

Tell us the truth of how you really feel inside the head of the untouchable you.

Open your heart to the truth of God.

There's no need to hide the untouchable you.

Let God touch you so that every hurt and pain that you try to hide will be healed and fade away.

You use your pride to shine like the sun.

The mask of pretence is your friend; a facade of many you are.

You hide behind the mask of another, transforming and conforming, the untouchable you.

If only you knew we would love the real you.
"Stop hiding"
I say, and be the touchable you!

Database

♥

How honest are you in your walk today?

How true and kind are you?

Do you have space in your heart for the truth of God to reign?

Do you declare the truth in your works?

It is said that ninety-nine and a half just won't do.

If God was to look in your database, what errors would He see?

Were you honest with your tax returns?

Your disclosure on your insurance forms?

Working and claiming benefits?
Driving without due care or license?

Check your database.
Is there anything that you haven't declared?
Be prepared to be contrite to put things right!
If God were to check your database, what would He see?

When My Door is Shut

S*UCH TORMENT, TURBULENCE, TROUBLES, tribulations!*

How much can I bear when my door is shut?
I cannot see clearly: no exit in sight!
No windows and no fire escape to take my flight.
My door is shut!
My door is shut!

Should I lay down in all this trouble and strife?

Turbulence, troubles, and tribulations all say "yes."

They are the majority; I hazard a guess.
I'll stay with them in their comfort zone.
They are all in agreement, I'll have you know.

Then the torment comes in and I'm restless again.
Is there no end to the 4 Ts again?
My door is shut, my door is shut!
Calamity snorts, "What a shame, such a shame!
To see one so holy with no outlet or key to get out of the situation that besets thee."

What they construed cannot be dismantled.
Alas, they shut my door!
"Peace be still," I hear a shout!

Torment, Turbulence, Troubles and Tribulations all fall down.

They were once powerful soldiers on the battleground.
Shooting their arrows along with their frowns.
As I tried to hide from their darts, I fell down.

Peace, peace! I raised my drooping head to see, the light of God resting on my weariness.
All doors flung open with the power of God.
Shut doors, locked doors?
Never to be seen again!

Anger

♥

Why speak from an angry place pouting words of disgrace that you cannot replace?

Why use venomous words that burn to the core through the bone into the marrow? Oh, the pain!

Each step I take brings pain, shame, and disgrace.

Those words hurt more than a knife sunken into the depths of my heart.

It brought me down so low.

Each word burned my soul, feeling like grime at the tip of your toe.

Is your slate clean as you let off your steam?

We have all fallen short on this journey called life while battling realms unknown.

Blinded by your pride you never saw the hurt inside of me.

Instead, you stood in glee laughing that you got one over me.

Words cannot be returned once they are out; they only hurt and damage the soul.

Choose your words wisely when you are angry and out of control.

Use self-control as your key.

Our Father above will take over when you give Him your all.

Take heed lest you lose someone close who is faithful, kind, and true as words said in anger can never be repealed.

Stop, think, and re-think your words.

Will they be words that your own heart will reject?

Use words that soothe the soul, that bring peace, love, and joy.

Think carefully about the words you choose to use.

Are you prepared to stand alone when all around you scatter?

Your tool of mass destruction has damaged many souls.

Behind your back they whisper, healing from the blisters you inflicted on your prey.

Ponder on these things.

The words that spring from your mouth: will they kill or will they heal?

The Trap

♥

*T*HERE IS A SNARE *that the enemy sets, for each and every one.*

To take us away from the truth and all the blessings that it brings.

The trap allows for decay to set in and slow death begins.

This is a terrible thing!

It starts in the mind where he conjures his lies, deceit, deception, and all the dastardly demise.

That allows you to imagine vain and atrocious things.

Then you make them your reality.

Meditation upon such topics will, of course, lead to decay.

Grasp hold of the lies and deceitful things that are lying in wait for you.

Inform the enemy of your soul that you are a follower of the King of Kings.

My Mountain

♥

I HAVE A MOUNTAIN *that is high and wide where rivers overflow in the valleys below.*

A mountain so wide that it is impossible to divide: too high to separate from the sky.

No matter what I try, the answer is still the same.

I have a mountain that I cannot divide.

It stares at me from its lofty place with stares of gladness, it doesn't hide.

It gloats with glee, as it knows I cannot flee from its strong, stony arms that always surround me.

Relentless is its name, relentless is its game to hinder me from my destiny.

"Oh, no! Oh no"!

A voice on high exclaims, "Let your mountains be removed in Jesus' name"!!!

My Pain

♥

MY LEGS HAVE REFUSED *to hold me up.*
The strain on my knees has given way to the pain.

I can no longer stand, as gravity pulls me down and down.

The weight is too heavy to bear.
I no longer see the hills as my sight is blighted by criticism and rejection.
"You're not good enough!"
Shame and despair profane.

Is this what you have gained from all the years of trying to walk on the narrow path that leads to glory?

How long? How long do I have to stay on this journey?

Only darkness follows me wherever I go.

The light flickers here and there, a glimmer of hope.

I reach out my hand to touch the light, but it dims as it sees me in sight.

How long? How long must I wait?

Is this my portion?

I am weary and in pain.

I can hardly lift my head off the ground, but I must hold on.

If I leave this earth on my account.

I've been told that darkness overshadows my destination.

That place is filled with sin and shame and unending degradation.

Where the light of God will never shine.

So I wait!

When I Am Weak

WHEN I AM WEAK, *He is strong.*
When I am lonely, He is my company.
When I am down, He picks me up.
When I am hurt, He heals me.
When I feel unloved, He loves me.
He wipes my tears.

When I feel rejected, He overshadows me.
When my finances are low, He sustains me.
When my mirror tells me
"You are hideous!"
His Word tells me:

I am beautifully and wonderfully made in His Image.

Who is this man?

JESUS!!!!

Forgiveness

♥

I'VE LEARNED THAT LIFE isn't easy; that there are only a few that you can trust.

When someone close hurts you it's a devastating loss.

I've learned to forgive and move on from the emotional pain and strain.

Understanding that I am not perfect and have hurt others too.

The love of God knows no bounds, His love is endless.

So, I extend this love to those who have hurt me and to those whom I have hurt.

True forgiveness overlooks all wrongs!
It allows you to love again!

Mind Decay

♥

Why do I allow it?
Why do I keep falling?
Why do I allow it?
Why do I keep falling?
Why do I allow the enemy to use my mind to distort the truth of who God is and what He can do?

He made a way through the Red Sea.
He crumbled the Jericho wall.
He protected the three Hebrew boys from the fiery furnace.

I know He will protect me.

So why do I allow the enemy of mind decay, to keep filtering through me?
My faith grows weak.
How quickly I forget the promises You made to me!
I allowed the spirit of mind decay to supersede what You instilled in me.

I call an end to the decay of my mind, which brings poverty and degeneration to my health.
Your attempt to work from within to use the things that are sensitive to me, to dismember me.
I call an end to mind decay.
There will be no delay in the things that God has for me.

My mind is made up:

No delay,

No decay,

No dismay,

No degeneration,

No disrepair.

My mind is not your battleground!

HBRCB

♥

*R*EPENT! REPENT! JESUS IS *coming sooner than you think!*

Heaven is a home built for you and I.

A home where peace will reign, and all sorrows will die!

"How can I get there"? you may ask.

Yes, this I can tell you, no fee, no charge!

You cannot get to heaven with sin!

The fearful, unbelieving, abominable murderers, whoremongers, sorcerers, idolaters, and liars shall not enter.

Confess with your mouth and believe in your heart that Jesus is Lord.

Ask Jesus to forgive you of every sin.

He died on the cross so that all can enter.

"How can I get there?"

You ask yet again.

I state this once and once again!

Confess with your mouth and believe in your heart, repent of your sins and Jesus will enter!

So, choose today to HBRCB!

What is this you say?

I say again...

H- hear the Word of God

B- believe He is Lord

R- repent of your sins

C- confess with your mouth that

Jesus is the son of God

B- be baptised for the remission of your sins

That is how you can win!

Take The Limits Off

♥

Why limit God if you know He is Lord?

Why settle for less when you know He is the best?

He made the world. He is limitless.

He's not about to be boxed up or remotely controlled, like a Jack in the box.

That comes out at a tap, at your will and your command.

Really? God can only move on a bishop's command, elders, or prophets.

Haven't you heard?

He can use anyone or anything to accomplish His will.

He has used a donkey to communicate.

He used a whale to imprison.

Take the limits off, it will profit you the most.

Do you think that when you get to the end of the road that this is the end?

When you take the limits off, the road continues to bend.

New avenues, roads, motorways, and highways.

He will always make a way where there is no way.

Take off the limits, and expect the unexpected.

Do not stay within your own limitations.

Stay away, from the temptation of sharing your goals with friends.

They have holes like sieves, which will kill your dreams, and they scheme.

Take off the limits and give the blind sight so that they can taste and see the goodness of God.

The lame will walk, the dumb will talk, and cancer will be healed at the touch of His hand.

So much can be achieved once you take the limits off.

Are you ready to lift off?

5...4...3...2...1

Scoff

*S*HOCKINGLY AND MOCKINGLY, YOU *treated me with such disdain.*

No encouragement or worthiness was seen at your door.

I came to you for support, but this was your rapport.

Scoff!

I supported you in everything when you thought that you had all things.

When the chips were down, I became your clown dancing at the beat of your feet.

When you were down and wearing a frown, and life ebbed from your heart.

I gave you a bed so that you could rest your head.

I lifted your heavy burdens so that you could have rest.

When you were hungry, I fed you.

When you were naked, I clothed you.

When you needed a shoulder to lean on, I was there for you.

I was all that you wanted me to be when you needed me.

I will be with you till the end, even though you are not my friend.

I see your heart, I hear your mind, I watched your actions and they are not pure.

I gave you undiluted love, and you gave me a stone.

When you love someone, you are with them to the end.

I hope you succeed in life, and that everything that you yearn for will be given to you in plain sight.

All I have is love for you, even though you scoffed and scorned me.

I will always be here for you but remember this: my arms will not continually be open to you, if you should ever come again.

Since you left me for dead I was fed with riches in glory and on this earth.

I was blessed with rivers flowing, North, East, South, and West.

God gave me the desires of my heart, which were His desires, too.

They say when you bless others that blessings will follow you.
All your scoffing and scolding propelled me to a new level, achieving the unachievable!
So today I say to you, I soooo
Thank you for your SCOFF.

The Graveyard Shift

♥

T*HEY SAY IT'S MY choice and my body.*
Then it should have been your choice to safeguard your housing from all harm and danger.

We often allow the passion to overtake our sense and sensibility.
A few minutes of pleasure is all it takes.
To make lifelong, sometimes devastating, decisions which can often last a lifetime of regret.

Where U turns are no longer possible.

If only I listened, if only I prayed, if only I followed what the good book says.
I almost lost my life. I should have been dead.
Even in my sin-soaked state, God remembered me.
He did not allow me to die on the operating table for the mistakes that I had made.

I used to live in regret, with my hidden secret deep down inside. When babies cried, I knew I was doomed, as I had no womb.
This was because of the choices I made before I met the King of Kings.

Many are fortunate and many are not.
My stomach turned into a graveyard; a dark, desolate place.

There's no more to be said.

I found my release through repentance, deliverance, prayer, and praise.
I am healed from trauma, guilt, and shame.
Please think and rethink before you decide.
Please, do not dance to the tune of the graveyard shift.

My Heart Says Yes

♥

My heart says yes, but my mind says no.
Fear has built a mountain so high and to the earth below.
A passion so strong that I cannot let go.
My heart pounds as I hear his voice.

My temperature rises and the heat is intense.
I cannot let go. It makes little sense.
Help! I need help! It's all in the past.
The walls are closing in.

I'm all boxed in.

I'm not whole, almost out of control.
I'm frozen, I cannot speak.
His arms reach out to embrace me.
My heart says yes, but my mind says no.
My heart melts.
I just can't!

I'm frozen again.
I cannot melt.
I have to say no! and run to the safe space haven that resides in my head.
I dread the thought of saying yes.
To walk down the aisle and say I do.
The things of the past won't let me go.
I have carried it for so long, like a coffin on my back.
I need to be made whole.

I feel so cold.

My issues are compounded by hate; by the things I was subjected to as a child.
It locked me into a world of degradation.
I wasn't to blame because it was not my shame.

Being misunderstood is a continuous thing.
The same way that I wear a mask that hides the me that hides within.
My exterior depicts a strong, harsh woman.
Inside hides a beautiful rose waiting to bloom.

Then I found the key to my dilemma; the most powerful word that heals.
Forgive to be forgiven as directed by the Lord, in prayer.

Finally, my shackles are broken.

Now that I know the power of forgiveness, my fearful heart has melted.

The stains of life have faded into a bottomless pit.

My heart says "Yes!"

My mind says "Yes!"

And I say" Yesssss!"

Arrows of Lies

♥

They're painful, Lord, those darts.
What, when and why?
Who could it be that is so mean to spread those arrows of lies?

Is it a close friend or a distant foe?
Chinese whispers spread by malicious antagonists.
Why? Oh why, does it hurt me so?
The recipient of the message believed it.

Accused am I, from a secret source, unknown.

What is the purpose of this onslaught?
To kill and destroy.
The blind leading the blind into a dark abyss filled with death and despair.

How humorous it is that human nature only remembers what it deems right in its sight.
No onus, on oneself, and the bitter melody commuted to others.
The screeching pain as the silent knife descends into my back.

Your command of the English language has allowed you to shift the blame;
to etch yourself out of the picture as the blameless one.
Out of the picture and out of the frame.
It's a game of cat and mouse.
You are the cat and I am the mouse.

I often wonder who you are, shifting positions from Jekyll to Hyde.

You shift to the left and then to the right.

A crescendo written just for me, with your orchestra of hate not far behind.

Are there deep hidden issues you are fighting to hide?

The truth behind the problem that you project onto others.

"Who are you?" is my question, "Friend or foe?"

It appears you need healing from way down below.

I'm in a glass bowl, with the eyes of the blind leering at me.

Oh, Lord help me.

I put on my mask of perfection and step outside to hide the deep turmoil inside.

Not knowing who they are or where they came from.
The pain, oh, the pain!
I can't take much more.
It's eating me up from the inside out.
Lord, over to You, I cannot cling anymore.

It hurts, Lord, it hurts; help me hold on.
I've tried my best.
I am not a soloist in this concerto.
There is someone standing with me.
He told me He would never leave me.

"I guess you're not good enough."
That's what the enemy said.

The Lord is with me, so I will be strong and carry on.

Lord, heal me from all my wrongs.

Make me a better person as I go on.

Rising Sun

♥

I woke up this morning to the rising sun.

What a blessing it is to see a brand-new day!

The birds in their homes chirping to the glory of God,

As if they knew He had provided for them once again.

The scurrying of the squirrels can be heard as they retrace their steps to their buried treasure.

An eagle-eyed cat rustles the blades of grass as it creeps along.

Water cascading from the fountain makes a wonderful sound as it flows.

Like the words of the Saints who give praise to God from the depths of their hearts.

I thank You for the dirty plates that housed the steak, pies and beans.

I give thanks that we have food to eat, as little or as large as it may be.

I thank You for the hands that fed the poor.

For the comfort, You gave to those who are forlorn.

Thank You for the ability to speak even though we may not be eloquent in speech.

My vision may not be 20\20, but I can see clearly through the midst of any storm.

The activity of my limbs can be painful at times but I can still move.

This is such a beautiful thing.

Thank You to my friends and enemies that keep me on my knees.
Thank You for my disorders, as You can put them in order.
You are the revealer and I know You are my healer.
You are my defence lawyer when I stand accused.

The rising Sun warms my heart and gives me all the vitamin D I need.
The Sun protects me from all antibodies and viruses.
He rebuilds my immune system and gives me the strength I need.

I need the rising Sun.

He is anything that I want Him to be.

He gives life and hope in gruesome times.

In desperation and depression, He comes to my rescue.

My rising Sun, my Love, my Father, my Doctor, my Lawyer, my Way-Maker, my Friend, and my great I am.

I can call on my rising sun any time of the day.

Today I call Him my rising sun as He woke me up.

Many of you know Him as Jesus.

How would you describe Him to someone today?

What You Hear!

R EMEMBER, YOU CANNOT BELIEVE all that you hear;
The lies that distort the truth and the fears.
It's progressive and suppresses the good and the truth.

It fills your head with grave decisions, so, what's the use?
Gossips spread fungus, disease, and unrest.
Do you really want to be put through this test?

To unclutter your mind from the drudge and the sin.

Is such a long process wouldn't it be better not to let it in.

3am TTJ

♥

It's 3 am. I still cannot sleep. I'm far too tired to count sheep.

Tossing from the left to the right, no peace in sight, I've seen every hour on the clock.

Lethargy hangs over me like a heavy weight.

I cannot say I woke up, as I never fell asleep.

The day has started.

My eyes sweep the floor, wishing that the hard concrete would be my bed.

I would use the raised pavement slab to be my pillow.

The Autumn leaves would unify and cover me.

Even then, sleep eluded me once again.

Then with the thought of the night air to comfort me.

I spoke to the moon and the stars and waved to Saturn and Mars.

Still, sleep eluded me.

I tried the stars covering the moon as my pillow.

The smell of the sea breeze and the sound of the waves and the melodic serenade whispered.

Still, sleep eluded me.

Concoctions for sleeping and teas of all kinds still didn't work for me.

Just like the Autumn leaves, my skin withered.

My eyes resembled two deep black holes with dense black gold so rich.

How wealthy would I be? If this were true.

However rich, sleep is all I need.
So many nights, no peace, no sleep.

Since the trauma, my life has turned slightly upside down.
The headaches were so strong, no pain relief was found.
A torrent of pain was raging in my head, filled with tears.
This pain lashed against my skull.
As a wave hits the rocks, to get to shore.

Barefoot was I while strolling in the dewy air the cool of the dew under my feet.
Each step crunches the decaying leaves and sends the ants scurrying to find new homes.

Then from the depth of the forest, a doe bleated my name.

Then suddenly I was face to face with antlers that seemed to last forever, almost touching heaven.

She bellowed to me.

Shock and trauma.

A cricket chirped, "Prayer is the key.

Talk to Jesus" (TTJ).

So much can be achieved when you relay your cares and pray.

His presence is like a muscle relaxer, counteracting the plans of the enemy.

The lack of sleep will destroy your immune system causing you to become weak.

The virus, such as sin. will enter.

The only anti-virus is TTJ.

My journey through the honeycomb of love with Jesus is like raindrops from the heavens.

He spoke to me in my sleepless oasis.

He rendered every shock and trauma void.

"Use My Word as your strong tower so that the enemy cannot devour your sleep.

Immerse yourself in My Word.

Let it be written upon your heart so that in your dreams you will call upon Me.

My repose is now sweet, I now rest on the pillow of righteousness.

A mattress filled with peaceful waters flows to the throne room.

Where the angels of mercy dispense grace.

TTJ is the key to unlocking the heavens.

It's 3 am; no time to count sheep as I am asleep.

Sunday Morning

♥

*S*UNDAY MORNING, TIME TO *down tools.*
Housework is no more - minor cooking to be explored.

Time to replenish the joy of the Lord until it overflows into the unending stream to the far reaches of the earth so that others know Jesus lives.

I am dressed in my finest linen, made with fine silk and priceless stones.

This is the garment of praise that covers me from my head to my toes.

For the extension of life, I praise Him and for His continuous outstretched arms that embrace me.

When Monday was bleak, You made a way from the meddlers and gossipers.

Tuesday, brought misery and company, trials and testimonies.

Wednesday, was a day of wickedness and woes.

Thursday, thirsty debt collectors were at my door.

Frugal Friday, no food to eat.

Saturday, no home so I sat on the street.

Sunday no home, no food to eat, living on the streets.

Your Word says that You will supply all my needs.

Your tender mercies and your favour are upon me.

The outsiders looking in thought she's out for the count, TKO.

The garment of praise is what I have left.

The most precocious, priceless gift of all that takes me through every day of the week.

I feel the raindrops on my head.

The piercing icicles lodge in my bones.

My toes are no more, as they melted away on Saturday.

The garment of praise is my comfort and friend.

When all have abandoned me, You are the one who lifts the burdens.

Your strength and love sustain me.

You are my warmth when nights are bitter.

I can call out Your Name, Jesus!
I can sing praise unto You.
There has never been a time when You haven't comforted me and satisfied my soul.

Into Your house I will go on this snowy Sunday morning to lift up Your Name.
As You are not to blame for my calamities.
I surround myself with an army of praise.
I discarded the garment of heaviness and threw it into the wind.
Who captured it and propelled it to the far reaches of the earth.

I clothed myself in my priceless garment of praise.
Lifted up a shout that shook the heavens.
Lost in praise was I.

Suddenly, the glory of God devoured me, restoring all that was lost.

I can never be without my garment of praise.

Can you?

Deep In Despair Jesus Was There

*I*NEVER LOST MY grace when pain weighed me down.
When deep down in despair, You were there.

In the night's stillness, alone and no one in sight, Your powerful arms of love surrounded me so.

They held me tight until the breaking of day.
The sunlight of your love opened my eyes to the morning glow.

In my darkest hour, You were there,

holding me in the shadows of my darkest despair.

Gravel

♥

Just as gravel passes through my fingers, so has love.

Fear overtook me and shook me, overshadowed me, and outshone me.

I allowed it to overtake me.

The gravel's hardness was in my heart: afraid to love or be loved.

Learn how to love me was the key.

How could I look in the mirror when the person was not me?

Just an illusion of who I would like to be the strong, successful, beautiful me.

Men saw my vulnerability and used me as they pleased.

My gift of love was unwrapped too soon.

Broken bones I couldn't hide were tentacles that broke off inside.

The world saw a stony face coupled with a stony heart.

What was the reality?

My heart is soft, longing for love.

The fear of being hurt sets in, then a stony façade appears.

Tears and fears erode my heart; the gravel resurfaces again.

I cried out to the Lord.

He heard my cry.

He came to my aid and made a way.

It is easier now, but when fear steps in, minute gravel filters in.

My heart does not agree with it, so I cast it out.

The dam has been broken.

I see myself for who I am.

A princess full of gladness, love, and kindness.

My eyes are now open to the truth and the beauty that is within.

The gravel has now melted.

I am who God says that I am.

I Almost Let Go

♥

WEIGHED DOWN WITH SO *many trivial things I almost let go.*

Why trivial? you say because the God that I serve has always made a way.

I was at an all-time low like never seen before.
Depression had me bound.
Just calling my name would have me slain.
I tried my friends but they didn't understand.

They did not know what was in God's plan.
My eyes were open to the things of God.
However, others could not see.

I was in a world of my own.

Speaking languages unknown to man, God understood as only He could.
He took me to a place where I could be comprehended.
A realm where all languages are one.

I fell to the ground and cried out to God.
I'm falling and turning back to the world.
I was spiralling out of control far from shore.
No help or understanding could be found.

I planned to lie on my floor all night until the King of Kings spoke to me.
He took me to a room where I surrendered my heart, my good, my bad, and my ugly.

The enemy's onslaught dug deep into my bones, which weakened my very frame.

During this time, I clung to the thread of his heavenly garment.

My strength was renewed in an instant.

I cannot run away from my problems.
I must run to God.
I cannot change things but prayer can.
I cannot move mountains but God can.
I will not let go!

Stuck Waiting for Death

♥

I'M ALIVE IN MY cage, ravished by age.

I look out from my prison and see the world.

Autumn, Winter, Spring, and Summer pass me by like a roaring river.

My eyes are still in their sockets, but they may as well be in my pocket.

Cataracts have taken hold.

How I long to feel the warmth of the sun on my face!

Captive in the glove compartment of a large abode.

Only able to manoeuvre my large and small toes, not sure which is which.

They are a distant monument that used to wear shoes.

Often, I wonder how human I am.

I feel like an animal, having to wait for its owner to take them out.

Sometimes, they put my clothes on inside out.

When I try to say it's not okay, no one hears.

It's not fair: they don't care to do the job that they are paid to do.

One told me it's not their duty of care to make my breakfast.

STUCK WAITING FOR DEATH

They promptly left me deep in distress that ran so deep.

No food to eat.
Sitting in filth, where is the care?
Their eyes choose not to see the me, inside of me.
How can this be? I'm not dead.
I'm still here inside my head, feeling and seeing all that they do.

I wait for hours for someone to change me.
I call until I am weak, no help insight.
So mistreated, so in despair as no one cares.
When I was young, I pondered on the Word of God.

I hid His words in my heart.

I brought them out and recited them day and night.

It brought comfort and strength to me, so that I could endure all the degradation that was metred out to me.

The physical pain of mistreatment and misdiagnosis did not help me.

My mental health was challenged.

I drifted in and out of insanity due to the mistreatment.

The Word of God stood by me and beside me as I battled the ill-treatment of others.

The tears rolled down my face, filling many oceans.

His Word that I hid in my heart, brought me out.

God spoke to me and said the diagnosis will be on paper, but it will not come to pass.

Until this day, it is still on paper.

The prayers of the saints, are a sweet incense to God.

I may be stuck in this body that has partially given up on me.

I have ten different diagnoses but God has kept me.

He gives me the strength to go on even when I don't want to.

My life-line is in God and in the family, He gave me.

He uses them to bless me and meet my daily needs.

My mind is now strong.

I'm witty and sprite while stuck in this body, which is not my friend.

The Love of God will never end.

Dance of the Mind

♥

THE MIND IS A dangerous place where you fight for your life; a place where you live or die.
The two-step dance.
Two steps forward in faith and two steps backwards in fear.

Imaginations are rife, it can bring strife.
You narrate, dictate, reiterate and disseminate the lies.
Publishing the worst-case scenarios of your life, making them your reality.

The war in my mind pounds like a drum.

With every beat, the wire that surrounds my head, tightens its grip and strips my soul.
My hands reach up to stop the pain.
This was all in vain.

The heavy pressing upon my head doesn't want to leave.
The tug of war pulling me to and fro.
The heaviness, the pressing, the pain.
I'm suffocating.
I start spiralling down and down, wondering if there is an end.
It has to go! You cannot stay!
Lord breathe on me without delay!

Some weight has shifted, there is more to go.
I call out Your name.
It shifts, and goes into hiding;

Lurking in the shadows, waiting to pounce at the chance that I may give in.

He will not win, as allowing the already defeated foe to win would be a sin.
More prayer, and more praise are what I need.
A time to reflect on any dirty deeds that let the enemy in.

I searched and found some entry points.
My ungodly thoughts allowed me to fall.
The gateway I opened for the enemy to enter.
This caused havoc to my aching soul.

The tug of war of good and evil caused me so much pain.
However, I felt God's words wash over me.

The sword of truth sliced through the enemy dividing his every being to the four corners of eternity.

Intrusion

*Y*OU CAME INTO MY *life so unexpectedly, inventing your so-called love for me.*
My guard was down.
I assumed that there would be no deceit from a child of the King of Kings.

A kiss you asked for? In shock was I.
I left the world far, far behind.
A man of God would stoop so low to allow pomposity to deplete him so; to spin webs of deceit to all you meet.

Not all that glitters is gold.

His smile was deceptive and so was he.

Only the eyes of the wise could see what was behind the masquerade.

A mastery of deception, that drew everyone's attention.

Fooling the hearts of many did not cost you a penny.

The trail of trampled flowers you left behind:

with a smile you wagged your tail of deception.

Onto the next victim, new territories to conquer.

You sat high and looked down below, thinking Job well done"! I have won"!

The webs of deceit were ever so sweet.

To see the ants beneath scrambling at your feet you practised weaving and deceiving.

They were so believing.

Remember, remember, that the things that you do will come back to bite you too.

Into the hands of God, I commend you.

Forgiveness is the key to moving forward from the pain of deception.

Thank you for showing your true colours.

Thank you for opening my eyes.

Thank you for the road map that I will not follow again.

Expecting to pick up where you left off, you rang my phone again.

We are like delicate flowers that need to be treated with loving tender care.

There will never be a time that you will have the power to intrude in my life again.

Broken Pitcher

♥

M*Y PITCHER IS BROKEN*: *I am so distraught.*
I cannot carry water and there is no draught.
The water is plentiful: my pitcher is gone.
I am thirsty and faint and cannot go on.

What has become of my life?
I have worked so hard for the Kingdom.
Read my bible every day.
Loved my enemies and gave money to the poor.

My pitcher is broken.
I am undone, lost, and bewildered.
Alone, bedraggled, far from anything I know.
Destined for a life of brokenness.

It was ceramic, broken into pieces unknown.
Impossible to piece together again.
Large and small portions are scattered in the stream.
Some flowing into the sea.

I glued together a crack that began as a split.
I covered the pieces with concealer that matched so well.
I slipped and fell on a stone of sin.
This started a descent into rivers that spiralled to Gehenna.

The truth became a lie and a lie became the truth.

I allowed the sins of the flesh to override my sense and sensibility.

I descended into depths unknown.

They were able to intimidate me.

So many compromises, I became so fragile.

There was no way to resist the temptations.

Several voices spoke together in harmony, willing me to sin.

My crimes were revealed to me.

They came to kill me.

"You have unforgiveness, lies, jealousy, theft and so much more".

"We have you now!

There is no turning back.

There is no way you can get back on track.

For the years you spent fighting against us, it's time to pay back".

They discussed the multiple times their plans had been thwarted.

They waited, plotted, found my weak spot: and executed their plan to destroy me.

Using concealer to hide my sins was not in God's plan.

There must be truth in the inward part.

Sin is not to be concealed.

The cracks cannot be made whole unless the Master takes control.

I was weak and, weighed down by sin, unable to fight against it.

Death was upon me.

My breath was about to leave my body.

I saw my sins before me.

I laid in total fear.

Chariots of fire surrounded me.

A heavenly brigade blew breath into me.

I repented of all my sins and Jesus resuscitated me.

He gave me a second chance.

This is one thing that the enemy has no capacity to do.

Defeated, the enemy was sent back to the abyss.

I have a new lease on life, which is dedicated to God.

I am now in His love and blessings.

As long as I stay close to His word in prayer, He will surround me with a fence of love, unending faith, and hope.

Charmed By Evil

♥

He came as a knight filled with so much might and delight.

As if made by the hands of God himself, His body was a picture of perfection.

His voice sent tremors through my bones when he spoke.

His face was a picture of precision, every contour specially designed.

His tones would send your imagination to a whole additional dimension of science fiction.

His eyes were light brown, and beamed like the sun at night.

They would light up a dark room.

Super distraction, as your imagination was sent to realms unknown.

He had an arm span that would have been able to encompass you three times over.

You know, in times of fear, those arms will wipe away every tear.

His shadow would cover a room and protect you from sunlight.

This man exuded an unspeakable charm that one could not ignore.

He gave me such a powerful light that left me breathless.

As a woman, I thought myself most favoured to have such a catch to speak to me.

I felt significantly honoured.

In the darkest hour of my life, I thought he was my light.

Someone with whom I could marry and have children.

I was unaware at the time that the Devil comes in delightful packages.

I said yes to his charms, as he wormed his way into my heart.

My senses were abducted, and I was taken to a timeless place where I wasn't sure there was ever a way back.

When his cheeks touched mine, they ignited a torrid passion deep in my soul.

I surrendered all my senses to the passion that was enthused within.

Eventually, I saw the demon, fused with drugs, alcohol, abuse, torment and sin.

I ran as fast as I could, only to find that the seed he planted began to grow.

I was told he needed a father, however, I thought "Never! Never!"

Pressure made me give in.

I allowed his charm to re-enter.

His true colours came out: a tirade of blows rained down on me.

One of them caught the baby; the others nearly blinded me.

As a punching bag, rather than a boxer, I took part in the match.

I knew then I danced with a demon and he was not my friend.

His own self-righteousness made him think he had won the grand prize.

He stood up proudly in celebration of it.

Having conquered Mount Everest, he thought he'd reached the summit.

I knew then that I had been charmed by evil.

As I thought about how to eliminate him, many thoughts came into my head.

I was prepared for the hitman to take him out.

However, I remember the teaching of Sunday school.

"Thou shall not kill."

So that thought was void.

The terrorization never seemed to end.

I didn't know what to do.

I had a praying mother who called upon the Lord.

He answered her and said, "Your terror will be no more."

He tried to venture near, so I disappeared to a place of safety under the shadow of the Almighty.

The Lord called out to me.

"Give your heart and life to me".

I yielded to the call and gave Him my all.

Charmed by evil, NOT I!

The Crushing

♥

THEY TOLD THEIR LIES.

Chastised was I, my record blemished without repeal, made to suffer by another.

Their venomous tongues spread poison rapidly, inducing bodily disharmony.

Talked about and despised as they told their lies, they pronounced me guilty!
I felt so filthy, like a leper.
I hid away from humanity.
I couldn't find my dignity!

I can declare this was not the case.

I was found guilty before the trial.

Innocence was my defence.

She looked at me directly in the eye, while smiling, she lied and lied!

Assuming that the deed was done!

The nails driven into the coffin, waiting for the undertakers to lower my casket, for the dust to meet the ashes.

Friends I thought I had, spun their webs of deceit.

As they thought it would be neat to sit below the boss's feet.

Feeding all their lies and treachery, using their charm to gain irresistible promotion from the boss.

Is this part of your plan?
To kill, steal and destroy?
Do you know that promotion comes from God and not from man?

No one was on my side.
Cemented on paper, the verdict was out.
Two years on my record and it wasn't my fault.
The deed carried out was not by me, but by another.

A hostile environment was designed, especially with me in mind.
A high price to pay for my innocence.
Persecuted, rejected and ostracised, something had to be done!

I challenged the decision.
The meeting was fierce.

I was on the losing ground.

I was about to give in when suddenly a sweet aroma filled the room.

The hearts of men were changing.
Fresh winds swept in like a precious gift.
Restitution was on the table.
Shush! The amount was not to be disclosed!

The funds came forth, but the indictment was already out!
Recorded in black and white.
The Lord gave me favour, as I did not waver, in the love that I know He has for me.

I learned to forgive; this was a difficult thing.
God changed me.
He re-arranged me, took my anger, and forgave me.

I asked Him to look at me and not at those who hate me.

By asking God to change me, He turned every curse against me superseding my expectations.

There is always elevation when we wait upon the Lord.

Break me Lord

♥

Transform me into the *person you want me to be.*

Break my bad habits and everything in me.

The tongue in my mouth must be broken from lying.

Break my stony heart so that I can love again.

Break every chain of unforgiveness; the anger within me and its dangerous streak.

Break off the shackles of jealousy and envy.

Break through the spirit of overthinking and let me live again.

Break the pride that guides my thoughts and actions.
Resentfulness, ruthlessness and restlessness.
Break me, Lord!

Look To God

♥

Look to God when you are feeling lonely.

Take your time to look to Him in times of sadness.

Looking up to God is the best thing you can do when you're in a desperate situation.

Take comfort in the presence of God when depressed.

When you are in a state of brokenness, look to God for comfort.

Despite the lack of money in the bank, still praise Him.

Disobedient children, look to God as He is your refuge.

Look to God in times of lying.

If you have lost someone close to you, look to God as your comforter.

In case of family disputes, look to God for strength and guidance.

When you find yourself in a state of sickness, pray.

When you don't have a roof over your head, look to GOD.

When you do not have any food to eat, look to God.

When you feel as if nothing is going right, all you need is GOD.

Let us, in all things, praise GOD and look to Him for everything.

The Poison Tongue

♥

The tongue is a two-edge sword: it can cut, devour, dismantle, dismount, desecrate, dislodge, dispose and destroy.

The tongue is unruly and can truly destroy a home.

Relationships crumble under its lash.

A pen, with ink that doesn't dissolve, leaves a stain that causes excruciating pain.

The whispers of lies and rumours, to boot, spread like wildfire with scars that run from the root.

It's like a bullet or pellet that shatters the mind, body and soul.

We should never find the poisonous tongue in our hearts or our thoughts.
Before you speak, will it lift or bring down?
What is your motive for your poisonous tongue?
To pull down, to tarnish, to block and stop
the fulfilment or the blessings of another?
Why bother?

Gossips and slanders God despises.
Use your tongue to bless and pray for one another, not to gossip and break confidence.
Take your eyes away from others.
Look to God, there is no other.
Turn your eyes inwards.
What do you see?

Twisted bitterness and low self-esteem.

Why and how do you know so much about other people's faults and many failures?

Do you eavesdrop at doors and windows and travel through realms unknown?

Is it a bid to take over the hearts and minds of men?

Do you want to control all those that you meet?

To be the wife of Ahab that is not neat.

Let your tongue turn on the light of God to everyone you meet.

Speak life into a deadly situation.

Encourage those who are lost and win their hearts to the cross.

Uphold the Word of God and destroy your toxic tongue.

Fall in Love

♥

*F**ALL IN LOVE WITH God this day and give yourself some love.*

You deserve all the love and attention that only God can give.

Connect to God, plug into the source, read the book of Love.

The Bible has all the information that you will ever need.

Treat yourself to peace, love, joy and so much more.

You should taste and see what He has in store for you.

He will energise your soul and make you glow like, the only star in the sky, as you are the apple of His eye.

Specially made with you in mind, happiness, peace, and joy.

You will become a new creation as reading His word allows all things to pass away.

He made you in His image so that you would not diminish.

He knitted you together in your mother's womb, and made you wonderful.

Fall in love with God today.

Do not delay, be the light in this world of darkness.

His plans for you are awesome.

He is about your welfare and gives you future hope.

He will always supply your needs as He has endless riches in glory.

Delight yourself in Him and He will give you the direction you need.

Fall in Love with the King of Kings.

In my lifetime, I never imagined that I'd see the day.

When there were multiple issues that ensued my soul.

It was then I turned to the duvet ministry.

Praying that things would improve.

I entered the boxing ring for another day of blows.

No matter how I dodged and tried not to fall the last blow knocked me out.

I couldn't move or make a sound, paralysed and on the ground.

I'm on my way to the cemetery without a doubt.
My funeral was arranged.
The headstone was laid.
I gave my last shout: Lord, I'm slipping away.
I cannot serve You anymore.
I'm too weak to hang on to the hem of Your garment.

Then from the height of the heavens, a ladder descended at my feet.
It lifted me up amid the clouds, and surrounded me.
It was as if my head was resting on a bed of peace.
Then a voice spoke softly from the clouds and said "You are down but you are not out!"

Mr Arrogant

♥

Your pride in yourself is exhaled as your own importance is inhaled.

Your head is held high as you strut around the domain with exaggerated self-importance.

You think you are the master of all.

Howbeit you are master of none.

The simple rudiments of manners have long gone.

The self-made title of your vain imagination is operating your cranial core.

You view others with such disdain that your own body flinches as they call your name.

You walk around with your head in the clouds, forgetting those who you hurt below.

The unforgiving words that you throw with each blow of your leather tongue.

Your vocabulary is such that you manipulate words.

The dance of your grammar indicts those in your throes.

Twisting the truth, you are so bold.

You also pretend that the souls you offend are under your control until the end.

As for your reputation, it has the same rhythm: arrogant, proud, unfaithful, and condescending.

Your reputation is important to you, but little do you know it is tarnished.

It vanished the day you put God down and took up your crown.

Your form of godliness keeps you on the outskirts.

The deeper things of God you are unaware of.

Let go of your crown, and remove the cobwebs from your knees.

Give all to God and lay all at His feet.

Allow Him to heal the broken places where the light of God has not shone.

He can change your name from Mr Arrogant to Mr Sincere.

I Woman

♥

L ET ME GROW FROM *kindness; I am a woman.*

I am like a flower that needs sunlight and warm rain.

I require love to be poured into me to sustain my growth.

Many have trampled on me and left me for dead, but I woman will never be buried.

The roots of my life must be nourished by love, kindness, and compassion.

I am like the beautiful orchid on the verge of blooming.

My light can illuminate the horizon for all time, and I can glitter like a star, until I reach the end of time.

I am reserved for those who are rich in love, whose hearts are warm and bold.

I am stunning, strong, vivacious, and courageous.

The I woman in me will support you until the bitter end.

This is my trend: to love undeservingly, on me one can depend.

I, Woman, am a vast collection of emotions for caring for those I love.

Blooming and growing do not pose any problems for me, if you really want to know.

The right combination of even temperament, time, patience, and devotion will provide the optimum growing environment.

I am rare, exotic and tropical and not often found in your native land.

So, take time to know I woman before you take me to the throne.

Talk to the King of Kings and Lord of Lords.

He will tell you all you need to know.

I woman can be eclectic while others are not so diverse.

Spending time to communicate is one of the important keys for growth.

Every I woman is awesome and unique.

All shapes and sizes, no DNA, is the same.

We bloom at different times.

With such uniqueness, through prayer and praise, there is one I woman that can bloom in your home all the years to come.

In times of exhaustion and weariness, I often have the appearance of being dead.

This actually isn't the case.

I woman is in a state of rest, getting ready for the blossoming of Spring.

I woman build our homes and will not tear them down.

We are precious; so much more than rubies and gold.

I woman is strong, reserved, with submissiveness to God who has ordained us till death do we part.

I woman is faithful, with an enormous amount of self-respect.

I will never lower my standards to conform to the rest of the crowd.

Secrets stay with me.

I wouldn't dare to share what others have entrusted to me.

Why I, woman, you might say?

Because I am whoever you want me to be; the multiple hats.

I am expected to wear as mother, wife, nurse and so much more.

I am whatever is required of me.

I woman.

Help Me Make It Through The Night

♥

INSIDE MY STOMACH, CHURN stomach-churning thoughts.

The rejection of the one you love most causes heartache and so much pain.

Your hopes built up so high and then brought down and crushed as if non-existent.

Amid this constant pain, every day that passes just seems to fall into the next one.

Upon waking, the first thing I see is it, the thing that won't let me go.

The churning in my stomach is real, but the problem is unseen.

I cannot share my problem, as no one can be trusted.

If only I could share my heart, but my heart I have to guard.

Even to my closest and trusted friend, I can only partially impart.

I have carried this for so long that the fear is always near.

I am the greatest actress you see; my inner heart is just for me.

The frustration is so great I keep running through the gate.

The unspent heaviness deep inside is driving me insane.

There is nowhere to hide.

The fight is fierce: there is a piercing in my soul that I cannot control.

I ask like Paul take this thorn away.

Each time I cry and think it's done; the force becomes stronger and I cannot go on.

The fight is vicious. It would like me to cave in.

It attacked the body in ways that cannot be explained.

It came like a thief in the night and caught me unaware.

I would have fainted if it wasn't for my belief in You, my Lord.

I called out Your name.

I told You, my pain.

I left nothing out.

I told nothing but the truth, without a doubt.

The groanings that could not be uttered came into play.

On my knees, I stayed and prayed.

Hours went by: and the thorn was still there.

I was uplifted above my sorrow with these comforting words, "My grace is sufficient for you".

Rejected or Protected

IT'S ALL ABOUT PERSPECTIVE, rejected by a man or woman,

Is it because they are not your fit?

Or he or she does not see your worth?

He could have red flags that could be detrimental and harmful to your mind, body, and soul.

Were you rejected, or protected?

Qualified for a job role, passed all the tests, the job was given to a lesser person with little or no regret.

They didn't even pass the test.

I wonder what you may have been saved from?

18 hours a day workload?
Having to work 7 days a week?
The threat of redundancy or a 15,000 pounds a year pay drop.
Not the annual pay rise!

The house you wanted to buy had increased sky-high.
The other buyer could afford to top that and more.
Was it the one for you?
Is there a better one out there?

The car that is far out of your budget, what is your reason for putting yourself in so much debt with your account deep in the red.
Pockets dried to a crisp?

Is it so unreasonable to live inside your budget?

Is it such a disgrace to flow in grace and learn to be content?

It's a matter of perspective; you are not rejected.

You have been protected!

So Hard

♥

S*O HARD TO FORGIVE!*
 Lord, why is it so hard to forgive the wrong that others do?

Knowing that you have wronged others too, why is this so hard to do?
The wound is so deep it seeps at the thought of the hurt and pain.

To say I forgive is lip service to the highest degree.
The rest of me just doesn't agree.

Deep down inside, you know you HAVE to let it go.

Something that you cannot accomplish on your own.

Take hold of the cloak of heaviness that is holding you bound.

Let peace be restored and unlock the door of forgiveness.

I ask you, Lord, for Your guidance and grace to allow me to let go of the hurt and the pain.

It's Complex

♥

It's complex, Lord, the things I have to do.
My feelings are laid bare before You.

I trust you, Lord; in all, You say and do.
The complexity of it all sometimes overwhelms me.

I give you my heart, mind, body, and soul to do with it what You will.
I give to You my all as I know you will bring me through.

Lord, I ask You to move away everything that is hindering me.

That I can see, and hear distinctly what Your will is for me.

I know You have a plan for me, a journey with highs and lows.

You also have the best for me and this I know.

Lord, I ask You to turn my complexity into simplicity.

Shine your light into the darkness.

Let me smile once more.

Welcome To the Safe Space Room

♥

THE SAFE SPACE ROOM. Where prayer, praise, and worship take place, is a room where souls can rest in the anointing that flows down to the soles of your feet.

All prayer requests are taken to the throne room of grace.

Sealed lips that keep the requests of the saints at the feet of grace.

The place where we share our goals, prayers, and affirmations.

The place where blessings are poured out to the saints.

The place where dreams are restored and the truth is told.

The place where the word is a lamp under our feet.

The place where your strength is renewed.

The room where the gospel DJ performs and seamlessly introduces awesome vibes to energise.

There are no titles or formality as we are the children of the most-high God.

The room where mind, body, soul, and spirit, are saved from the dragon and his foes.

Where is this safe space room?

It is in the throne room of grace.

How do I get there?

Through prayer.

Praise to the King!

Welcome to the Safe Space Room!

Each Time

♥

*T*HE SUNLIGHT TO MY heart you are, and you will never know.

How much my heart yearns for you and you're only a stone's throw away.

Your voice is like a melody singing softly in my ears: not knowing what you do for me each time that you walk near.

My eyes are like spotlights each time that you draw near.

My hopes are dashed as you do not see me as I see you.

My knight in shining armour, rescuing me from my lonely pain.

My heart pounds each time you call my name.

I dream of you holding me in your arms but that day has not yet come.

Please come home to where you belong.

Should I tell you of my feelings or hold on and be strong?

Let patience be my witness and stand firm and just hold on.

People change, yes, they do, but that change seems too long.

The love I feel so deep down inside, can it be so wrong?

It grows like a river flowing out to the sea.

Never-ending, just flowing to the ends of the earth and beyond.

I cling to the hope that one day you will see me as I see you; that your thoughts will be my thoughts.

Our hearts will be entwined as one, reaching for the stars.

Each time I think of you, I pray my dreams to come true.

Alas, I wake up, and guess what?
It was just a dream.

Day One

♥

I LOVED YOU FROM day one.

   I loved you from day two.

I loved you on day three, but you were not true.

You made me so blue.

On day four, you knocked on my door;

I almost fell on the floor.

You declared your love for me.

On day five I had a surprise as you proposed to me.

On day six it was wedded bliss.

On day seven, I'm still in heaven.

I loved you from day one and now I love you forever.

Just a Smile

♥

JUST YOUR SMILE SENDS shivers down my spine.
The warmth of your breath heats my soul.
Your very essence vaporizers the air with a sweet-smelling fragrance of love.

My heart pounds so loud it is louder than the beat of a drum.
The touch of your hand tantalises me so my veins stand to attention, waiting to be released from the captive audience of your hand.

As you walked past, I brushed against your hair as you bent down to capture the butterfly.

My hand was drawn to you as a magnet, not wanting to let go.

Just your smile is all it takes to keep my love for you awake.

As you draw close to me.

I hear the thud of your heartbeat beating in time with mine as we flow and exchange love's pleasant glow.

A loud siren was heard, which I tried to ignore.

Louder and louder, it came with such distain.

I cannot be blamed.

I tried my best to find out his name.

The alarm was on its second ring.

I'll try again tomorrow as the parting is not a sweet thing.

Just One Question!

♥

*J**UST ONE QUESTION, IF I may, Lord.*

When will this loneliness end?

When will I be able to have and to hold to the very end?

When will the loving arms of the husband that you have chosen for me whisper Godly blessings through the still of the night?

He that finds a wife, finds a good thing.

Let me be that good thing.

I have waited so long for my godly spouse to be the head of the home, with all spiritual might.

The man that will put you first and be consistent, too.

He will detect, eject, and protect his home from every devilish foe when finances are at an all-time low.

During stormy times, wagging tongues destined to destroy, he will continue to magnify the Lord.

Someone forthright with no lying lips or Turkish delights.

To ignite the Word of God, to be a lamp under our feet.

I know the husband that You have for me is formed and made whole.

Every Time

♥

THERE IS SOMETHING IN *my heart that aches every time you tell me you're leaving.*
There's an uneasy feeling in my stomach that causes me to feel so ill.

I have been silently in love with you for as long as I can remember.
My heart is tender every time you are near; stars appear with just a touch of your hand.
Although it's difficult to hide my love from you, I must, because you don't see me as I see you.

When I daydream about you, I imagine how life would be if you held me in your arms.

In order not to speak about my feelings out loud, I battle daily for self-control.

Seeing your name on the screen of my phone as it rings shows a smile that radiates for 5 kilometres.

I feel so close and yet so far away at the same time.

I leave my love and emotions in the hands of God since it was not meant to be.

Love

I LOVE YOU MORE *than the stars above:*
   the moon that shines in the pleasant skies.
   You make me feel so brand new, with your encouraging smile which is born anew.

   The twinkle in your eyes as you watch me pass by.
   The tender touches that send shivers down my spine.
   Your soothing baritone voice that shivers the mountains.

The volcanic eruption within me: so I cannot speak about the love I have for you.

I freeze at the sound of your name.

My hair curls on its own accord every time you draw near.

The thought of never seeing you again brings pain.

Don't break my heart; stay with me and love me like you did before.

The hugs that seemed to last a lifetime.

The flowing compliments that lifted my soul.

Take time out and listen to your heart.

Just love me again.

I Want a Rich Man

♥

I WANT A RICH man, but not a man with money.

But he must have a little bit of funny.

I want a rich man, but he has to be strong to carry the weight of my love.

A rich man with an overwhelming abundance of respect for me would be ideal.

I want a rich man who loves God more than he loves me.

This means that I will know, for sure, that he truly, adores me.

I want a rich man, who knows how to make me smile through times of pain and sorrow.

I want a rich man, who is able to dissect the Word of God with me.

I want a rich man who flourishes in forgiveness.

When two become one there will be some misgivings.

Regardless of the issue, the sun should not set on anyone.

I want a rich man, that supports and encourages others.

I want a rich man, that is handsome from the inside out.

Not just eye candy, that would be dandy, but it is the heart of the matter that matters.

The heart speaks volumes.
It shows you who you are.
If the heart is right, the outside will be a delight.
I want a rich man. It's not about silver or gold.
It is the heart of the man that is the main currency for this transaction.

I want a rich man whose heart is full of love for God.
The one who wears the whole armour of God in the stillness of the night to detect the night prowler and to wield the sword of the Spirit.

It would be nice to have a man who is wealthy, but I prefer a man that likes to dwell in that secret place of the most- high.

Is that man you?

Scrapheap

♥

Why put me on the scrapheap when I have so much left inside?
You put me on the scrapheap.
Did you think I would die?

It is said that I will flourish and bear fruit in my old age.
Sit in the courts of my Saviour and never, ever waver.

The Lord is my rock and fortress.
He has placed me on higher ground.

He has made me in His image and keeps me in His will.

My exterior may be decaying but my interior is being renewed.

I am sharp-sighted and my perception is in the Lord.

I have the strength of a lion poured out on me each day.

God renews my brain cells in such a magnificent way.

He brings everything back to my remembrance and guides me when I pray.

How dare you put me on the scrapheap?

When the love of God has not grown cold.

The gifts of God will make room for me.

My wisdom, knowledge, love, and understanding.

I will take with me, and use them in a place that God will choose.

How can you put me on the scrapheap?

I'm not done yet!

I'm not done yet!

This will not discourage me.

I flourish,

I flourish,

I flourish, and I will continue to flourish in the place that God has destined for me.

The Sun will Shine Again

♥

T*HE SUN WILL SHINE again through the clouds and rain.*

Though the storms may blow and the wind of change hides his face, know that the sun will shine again.

The clouds may hang low and the tears may flow: the light of the sun may seem no more.

What crime have I committed to feel such pain?

Know this, the sun will shine again.

Doors close, but there are doors that are opening.

His grace abounds in the lowest valleys and mountaintops.

Know this, the sun will shine again.

On this day know this, God is love.

His love for you is endless and knows no time.

There are no storms that His love cannot subdue.

Know this, the sun will shine again.

Sugar Coat

♥

Y*OU SOLICITED THE SECRETS of others under the ruse of being their friend.*

They shared their innermost secrets, but for you it was just pretence.

Your insecurities about who you are, shadow the spirit of Jezebel.

That wink could start a nuclear war, without the strumming of your vocal cords that echo the sound of guitar strings.

Ravenous for attention, the pull is so strong.

It mimics the magnetic attraction of ferromagnetic metals.

You delight in the things of this world.

Maligning others. Why is this your concern?
Help us be perfect like you!
The road to perfection is difficult so, if you please, try to stay on your knees.

While you are there, look up in the air.
Pull down the cloud of vilipend, those words you have used as knives to pierce each soul.

Your deposit of love is a dramatic contrast to the person who we see.
Your fuel is the fire of internal unrest.

You want to be the cream of the crop.

However, this is associated with love, joy, and peace.

You hide behind this smoke screen.

Your hearts beat for another.

Your colours change just as swiftly as a chameleon.

You camouflage well, choosing your prey.

Dissecting the weak from the strong, carefully pulling the meat from the bone.

Dissecting the marrow from the bone.

Highlighting the weaknesses and not the strengths.

A minute and enlarged-looking glass collecting all the flaws.

As if fine dining, carefully slicing and dicing their innermost being.

Manipulating so sophisticated and yet... there is a flash of the emotion of care.

The direction of your mouth compass is always set to North, where icicles reign.

Jagged hail stones shoot like arrows from your mouth.

It is such a shame that you have deposited on others words that offend the soul.

This authority comes from the one who wants to steal our souls.

Take note! We are all flawed in areas that only God can mend.

Your sugar-coated venom will not last long.

As sugar melts with heat, the fire from your tongue will strip away your truth.

Exposed, you will be like the sun, lonely in the dark blue sky.

It is with great joy we announce that your journey on the express train of dogmatism has come to a close.

As you lay down your arms and rest from your tyranny, allow the love of God to melt your heart.

There is no longer any need for you to hold on to your weapons!

Your war is over!

Acceleration

♥

Good morning! It's your *acceleration day!*
Where God will take you to new heights.
He has already orchestrated your journey.
See how swiftly He has moved away your calamities.

Your promotion has already been written.
So, there is no question.
Step into your blessing.
There is a pressing.
New heights he has given to you.

You have received a magnificent gift from God.

To edify those around you and those who don't love you.

God's love is not partial.

The counsel you give changes the lives of those you encounter profoundly.

His love is eternal, that love he has given to you.

The embedded wisdom that flows from God is cemented within your soul.

Empty your heart continuously to God.

As out of your heart, the issues of life flow.

The greatness within you that comes from Heaven above is accelerating you today.

Printed in Great Britain
by Amazon

24940429R00096